Cat Got a Lot

I Like to Read® books, created by award-winning picture book artists as well as talented newcomers, instill confidence and the joy of reading in new readers.

We want to hear every new reader say, "I like to read!"

Visit our website for flash cards, activities, and more about the series:
www.holidayhouse.com/ILiketoRead
#ILTR
This book has been tested by an educational expert
and determined to be a guided reading level C.

Also by Steve Henry

Happy Cat

★ "This cheery entry in the I Like to Read series successfully tells a simple tale and creates a sense of community using just 20 unique words. . . . Plenty of visual cues, lots of repetition and a clear story arc make this a perfect choice for beginning readers."
—*Kirkus Reviews* (starred review)

Cat Got
a Lot

Steve Henry

I Like to Read®

HOLIDAY HOUSE • NEW YORK

For Shelley

I LIKE TO READ is a registered trademark of Holiday House Publishing, Inc.

Copyright © 2015 by Steve Henry
All Rights Reserved
HOLIDAY HOUSE is registered in the U.S. Patent and Trademark Office.
Printed and Bound in August 2019 at Phoenix Color, Hagerstown, MD, USA.
The artwork was created with watercolor, gouache ink, and brown craft paper.
www.holidayhouse.com

3 5 7 9 10 8 6 4

Library of Congress Cataloging-in-Publication Data
Henry, Steve, 1948-
Cat got a lot / Steve Henry. — First edition.
pages cm. — (I like to read)
Summary: "Cat goes out, and comes back with a lot of new things"— Provided by publisher.
ISBN 978-0-8234-3385-8 (hardcover)
[1. Cats—Fiction.] I. Title.
PZ7.H39732Cat 2015
[E]—dc23
2014032301

ISBN 978-0-8234-3419-0 (paperback)
ISBN 978-0-8234-3990-4 (6 x 9 paperback)

Cat liked fish.

He went down.

And he went down.

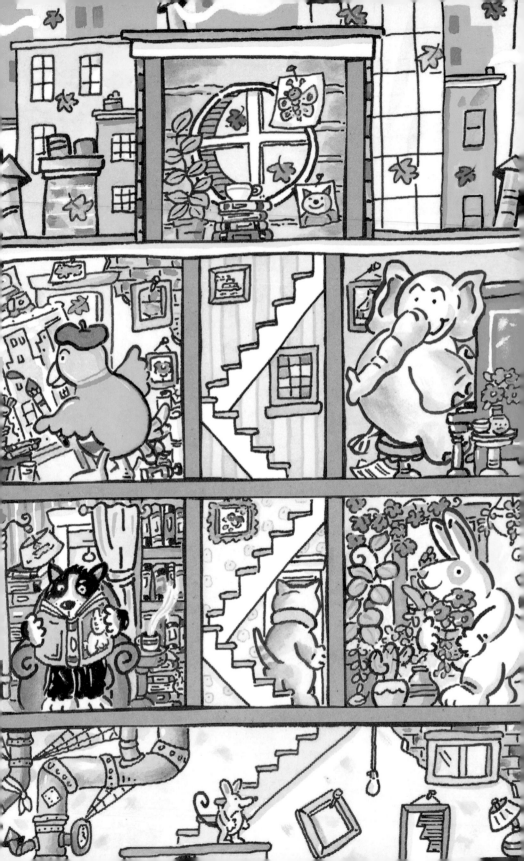

Cat went out.

He saw a horn.

He went in.

Cat went out.

He saw books.

Cat went in.

And he went in.

And he went in.

Cat went
back out.

And he went back in.

Then Cat went home.

All were happy.

And Cat was happy.

I Like to Read®

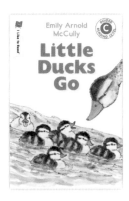

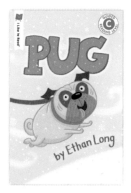

Visit http://www.holidayhouse.com/ILiketoRead for more about I Like to Read® books, including flash cards, reproducibles, and the complete list of titles.